Making Friends

with Samson

by Alison Peters

illustrated by Nathan Jurevicius

The Characters

Nathan
He really wants a dog.

Kevin and his gang
They're trouble.

Mum & **Dad**
They mean well.

The Setting

CONTENTS

CHAPTER 1

Nathan's Wish List

Nathan Clark had always wanted a dog.
When his family moved to the city,
it was all he could think about.

"We don't have a garden," said Mum.

"The city's no place for a dog," said Dad.

Nathan dreamed that one day they would change their minds and when they did, he would be ready.

He read books about dogs. He knew
what to feed them. He knew what to
do if they had fleas. He knew exactly
what he would do with his dog.

In his top drawer was his list.

Great Things to Do with a Dog

1. Take the dog everywhere, like fishing and to Uncle Bill's farm.
2. Teach it to sit.
3. Teach it to wait at the door for me.
4. Let it sleep beside my bed.

5

After a few days at his new school he added two more.

5. Teach it to fetch things like newspapers, sticks and baseball caps — after Kevin's gang has stolen them.
6. Teach it to scare off other dogs, like Kevin's dog, Killer.

He even picked out a name ... Samson.

CHAPTER

Nathan's Birthday

On his birthday Mum and Dad put a big box on his bed.

"Happy Birthday, Sweetheart," said Mum.

'Pete's Pets' was written along the side and there were holes along the top so a puppy could breathe.

"You'll be surprised," Dad smiled.

Nathan knew what it was. He held in an excited squeal as he lifted the top from the box.

He couldn't wait to meet his new, furry,
friendly, jumping, barking, tail-wagging ...

BIRD?! His dog was a bird! It couldn't bark or jump or wag its tail. In fact, it didn't move at all. For a second it didn't seem real.

"Oh," Nathan gulped. "I-i-it is a surprise."

It was a worse surprise than last birthday. Nathan had wanted a 'Super Simon' computer game, but found a book about boats on the end of his bed.

13

CHAPTER 3

Chirp! Chirp!

For weeks the bird sat silently staring at him. Nathan changed the water and seed every few days, but he didn't speak to it. What was the point?

Whenever he walked near the cage, the bird moved along the perch to get as far away from Nathan as he could.

One day, the bird cocked its head
to one side and made a small sound.
"Chirp," it squeaked.

"Was that you, bird?" Nathan asked.

"Chirp," the bird sang, then turned
upside down and spread its wings.

"So you can hang upside down. So what? You can't chase a stick or catch a ball. What good are you?" Nathan grumbled.

The next time Nathan came near,
the bird didn't move away.

Nathan moved closer to the cage.
The bird didn't move. Nathan put his
hand *inside* the cage. The bird still
didn't move. He tried to grab it and
... it bit him hard.

19

"BIRRDD!!!!" Nathan yelled, "You nearly bit my finger off!"

Frightened, the bird flapped inside the cage. Its wings crashed against the sides.

"Shhh," Nathan whispered, "Sorry bird. It's OK. Shhh."

Slowly the bird calmed down.

CHAPTER 4

Making Friends with Bird

Two weeks later, Nathan tried again.
Carefully he stuck his finger inside
the cage. The bird didn't move.
Nathan put his finger near the perch.
The bird HOPPED ON!

"Good bird," he whispered, "good bird."

Every afternoon they practised, over
and over and over again.

Soon Nathan could even take the bird
out of the cage. One night, the bird
flew onto Nathan's head. After he
checked that the windows were
closed, he wore the bird to dinner.

"You couldn't do that with a dog!"
said Dad.

"I suppose," Nathan shrugged. He
still knew a dog would be better than
a bird.

At school the next day, all Nathan could think about was the bird.

"What can I teach him next?" he wondered as he ate his sandwich and watched the boys playing with a tennis ball.

Just then, Kevin and his gang crept up.

"Got it!" yelled Kevin, as he swiped the cap from Nathan's head. It was his favourite cap, the old blue one Uncle Bill had given him.

Nathan sat in the library for the rest of the lunch break. Kevin and his gang never went in there.

At the magazine table he couldn't believe his eyes. On the cover of one was a photograph of a man, in black leather, riding a motorbike. Riding on the handlebars was a parrot.

It was trained to stay there as the bike sped along!

Nathan had an idea.

Bike Riding Lessons

After school he went out to the garage with the birdcage. He took the bird out and put it on the handlebars of his bike.

He rode the bike in a circle slowly.
Then he rode faster. The bird stayed
on!

The next day Nathan took the bird on his bike into the courtyard behind the block of flats. The bird didn't fly away.

Nathan rode the bike in a circle, faster and faster and *still* the bird held on. It was incredible!

Nathan was excited. He couldn't wait to show somebody. But who? Dad was doing an extra shift at the hardware shop. Mum was working at the café.

Nathan thought of the gang. He thought about Kevin. The bird needed more practice but it would be cool to show off their new trick. Nathan opened the side gate and took the bird to the park.

CHAPTER 6

Kevin and Killer

The gang was playing footy. Their bikes were under a tree. Killer and the other dogs were on guard duty.

He rode his bike slowly along the footpath. Maybe they'd notice. Maybe they would want to come and have a look. Maybe they'd be impressed. They might even let him play.

Killer saw the bird first.

"Grrrrrrrr." The gang looked up. Killer
pulled at his leash. The other dogs
barked. The bird froze in fear.

"Oh no," thought Nathan.

"No cap today, Nathan?" Kevin asked.
The gang laughed.

"Is that a plastic tweetie bird on your handlebars?" he teased.

The bird began to flap.

"Ooooh, it moves! HELLO COCKY," he yelled and grabbed at the bird.

The bird flew off the handlebars in
panic. It soared past the tree and
out of sight. Killer and the other dogs
went wild.

Kevin and the gang laughed, but
Nathan hardly heard them. He was
pedalling past the gang, past the tree,
past the dogs and into the wood
behind the park.

"I wish I'd never left the garage," he said to himself. He rode along the track, searching for his bird in the trees. It was no good. The bird was gone.

CHAPTER 7

Bird in Danger

Nathan could hear the gang playing footy again.

Just then Killer's ears shot up.
"Chirp! Chirp!"
The other dogs heard it too.
"Chirrrrup."
Oh no! It was the bird, perched on
a low branch just above the dogs'
heads. The dogs growled and snapped
at its tail feathers.

"Psst, bird," Nathan called desperately. "Come on bird."

But the bird wouldn't go to Nathan. It screeched and flew onto the seat of one of the bikes. The dogs were a barking tangle of leashes, tails and teeth.

The bird flew to another bike seat and then another. Finally it landed on Kevin's bike which was propped against the tree. Uncle Bill's blue cap was hanging from the brake handle.

Killer growled and jumped over the other dogs with his jaws snapping. His leash stretched tight.

"Oh no, he'll eat my bird for sure,"
Nathan thought.

Kevin ran towards the tree. Suddenly there was a yelp and a yell as Kevin tripped over Killer's leash. He flew through the air and crashed onto his bike. Killer landed on top. What a mess!

The other boys began to laugh.
Killer licked Kevin's face.
"Get off, you stupid dog!" Kevin
yelled. "What's that white stuff on
my bike seat?"
It was bird poo.

The boys laughed harder, but not
as hard as Nathan.

"That's a cool bird," said one of the boys. "How'd you teach it to do all that?"

"It takes practice. And a smart bird!" Nathan said as he grabbed his cap off Kevin's bike.

"Can you train dogs?" the boy asked.

"Probably," Nathan smiled. "But I like birds better."

That night, Nathan moved the cage
so it was next to his bed.

"Goodnight bird," Nathan said softly.
"You should have a proper name."

"From now on your name will be Samson."

Samson shook himself, ruffled his feathers and tucked his head under his wing.

GLOSSARY

courtyard
a small enclosed
paved garden

desperately
very nervous or fearful

exactly
every single thing spot on

extra shift
working double
the usual time

impressed
to think something is great

incredible
very hard to believe.

perched
sitting still like
a bird on a branch

propped
leaning against
something

ruffled
made his feathers puff up

searching
looking very hard

Alison Peters

What is your favourite breakfast?

Cold pizza and coffee.

Who is your favourite cartoon character?

Bart Simpson.

What was your least favourite activity at school?

Concentrating.

Why is the sky blue?

Somebody explained it to me in great detail once, but I can't remember a word of it.

Nathan Jurevicius

What is your favourite breakfast?

Muesli with chopped banana and green tea.

Who is your favourite cartoon character?

Felix the cat.

What was your least favourite activity at school?

Maths.

Why is the sky blue?

The sky is blue?